LUCY & TOM AT THE SEASIDE

LUCY AND TOM AT THE SEASIDE
A CAROUSEL BOOK 0 552 52144 2

First published in Great Britain by Victor Gollancz Limited

PRINTING HISTORY
Victor Gollancz edition published 1976
Carousel edition published 1981

Copyright © Shirley Hughes 1976

Carousel Books are published by
Transworld Publishers Ltd.,
Century House, 61 - 63 Uxbridge Road,
Ealing, London W5 5SA.

Printed in West Germany
by Mohndruck

LUCY & TOM
AT THE SEASIDE

written and drawn by

Shirley Hughes

A CAROUSEL BOOK
TRANSWORLD PUBLISHERS LTD.

One hot day Lucy and Tom and their Mum and Dad
thought they would go to the seaside.

Lucy is helping to pack up the picnic. There are sandwiches
and hard-boiled eggs, apples, biscuits and a bottle of orange
squash. There is also a lovely chocolate cake.

Tom goes off to find the buckets and spades in the sandpit.

They go to the seaside in the train.

Tom keeps asking when they are going to get to the sea.

Lucy wears her armbands in the train so as to be all ready to swim when they get there.

At last they've arrived! They walk down a rather long road carrying all the picnic things and bathing bags and buckets and spades.

There's a very special seasidey smell.

And there's the sea!

It's much, much bigger than either Lucy or Tom had ever remembered.

They run straight down to where the waves are coming up on to the wet sand and walk along the edge.

There are a lot of other children on the beach as well as mothers and fathers and babies and grannies and people paddling, and dogs who dash in and out of the water barking excitedly at seagulls.

Lucy and Tom want to bathe right away, so they all put on their bathing suits and go into the sea, hand in hand. Lucy and Dad do some swimming. The sea is much rougher and splashier than the swimming pool near home. It's harder to swim in, but much more fun.

Tom likes being chased by the waves.

After the bathe Mum helps everyone to rub dry and
they play a running-about game to get warm.
They settle down to their picnic.
Several wasps try to join in.

The tide is coming in.

Dad helps Lucy and Tom to make a beautiful sand castle. It has turrets covered in shells and stones, a moat, and a tunnel going right through the middle and coming out the other side.

Slowly the moat fills up with water, then the tunnel.

Soon only the top turret is left.

Then nothing at all.

A lot of interesting things are happening on the beach.

There are people flying kites and playing cricket and ball games.

Two little girls are burying their father's legs in the sand so that only his toes are sticking out.

Some people are trying to get in or out of their bathing suits under towels, which is very difficult.

Lucy and Tom play in a rock-pool.

Lucy finds lots of different kinds of seaweed and some shells

which she puts into her bucket.

Tom finds some stones and a crab's claw.

Lucy makes a face in the sand. It has stones for eyes, a row
of little shells for teeth, and a lot of seaweedy hair.
Mum helps Tom make a speedboat pointing right out to sea.

Further up the beach there are some donkeys. Lucy and Tom ask if they can have a ride.

Lucy's donkey is grey with white legs. His name – 'Pepsi' – is written on his harness.

Tom's donkey is brown and is called 'Sarsparilla'.

It's nearly time to go home.

Mum is packing up the picnic things.

There's just time for a last ice-cream.

Lucy writes her name in very big letters in the wet sand.

Then she writes Tom's name too.

It's been a *lovely* day.